DRAGON's Halloween

DRAGON'S FIFTH TALE

Dav Pilkey

ORCHARD BOOKS · NEW YORK

THE DRAGON TALES

Orchard Books, 95 Madison Avenue, New York, NY 10016

Manufactured in the United States of America
Printed by Barton Press, Inc.
Bound by Horowitz/Rae
Series designed by Mina Greenstein
The text of this book is set in 18 point Galliard condensed.
The illustrations are watercolor with pencil, reproduced in full color.
2 4 6 8 10 9 7 5 3 1

Library of Congress Cataloging-in-Publication Data
Pilkey, Dav, date.
Dragon's Halloween : Dragon's fifth tale / Dav Pilkey.
p. cm. (The Dragon tales)
Summary: Dragon has a busy and fun-filled Halloween, turning six
small pumpkins into one big jack-o-lantern, going to a costume
party, and taking a spooky walk in the woods.
ISBN 0-531-05990-1. ISBN 0-531-08590-2 (lib. bdg.)
[1. Dragons—Fiction. 2. Halloween—Fiction.] I. Title.
II. Series: Pilkey, Dav, date. Dragon tales.
PZ7.P63123Dsh 1993 [E]—dc20 91-21107

Contents

For Herb Sandberg

FREE
PUMPKINS

1
Six Small Pumpkins

It was October,
and all the world was orange and brown.
Dragon walked through the autumn leaves
in search of a giant pumpkin.

6

"I will find a pumpkin as big as a house,"
said Dragon.
"Oh, what a scary jack-o'-lantern
it will make."

7

But when Dragon got to the pumpkin patch,
all of the big pumpkins were already gone.
Only six small pumpkins were left,
and they were much too small to be scary.

Dragon loaded the six small
pumpkins into his cart
and brought them home anyway.

Later, as Dragon sat carving
his small pumpkins,
a fox and a crocodile came by.
"What are you doing?" asked the fox.

"I'm making scary jack-o'-lanterns,"
said Dragon.

"Those pumpkins are too small to be scary,"
said the fox.

"Just wait," said Dragon.

Dragon took one of the pumpkins
and poked branches into its sides.

"That pumpkin looks stupid,"
said the crocodile.
"No one will be afraid of your silly
jack-o'-lanterns!"

"Just wait," said Dragon.

Dragon put candles into the pumpkins,
and they all lit up bright and orange.

"Ha, ha, ha, ha, ha!" laughed the fox
and the crocodile.

"We've never seen such funny jack-o'-lanterns
in all our lives!"

"Just wait," said Dragon.

13

Finally, Dragon stacked the pumpkins
on top of one another
until they were very tall.
The fox and the crocodile
stopped laughing.
Their eyes became wide.
They began to tremble and shake.

"Ah . . . *aaaaah!*" cried the crocodile.

"Oh . . . *oooooh!*" wailed the fox.

15

The fox and the crocodile ran off
through the woods, screaming in terror.

"What's the matter with them?"
said Dragon.

Dragon scratched his big head and
looked up at the jack-o'-lanterns.
"Aaah! Eeeh! Aaah!" screamed Dragon.

Dragon ran into his house
and hid under the bed.

"I did not know
that six small pumpkins could be so scary!"
said Dragon.

2
The Costume Party

It was Halloween night,
and Dragon was very excited.
He had been invited to a
Halloween costume party.

Dragon tried to think of
a scary costume to wear.

Dragon could not decide whether to be
a witch, a vampire, or a mummy.
He thought and thought,
and scratched his big head.

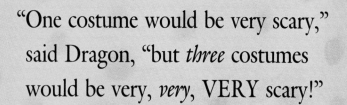

"One costume would be very scary," said Dragon, "but *three* costumes would be very, *very*, VERY scary!"

So Dragon decided to wear all three costumes at the same time.

First, Dragon put on
a witch's hat and nose.
"I feel scary already," said Dragon.

23

Next, Dragon put on a vampire's cape
and teeth.
Dragon could not talk very well
with vampire teeth in his mouth.
"Flmmm flmmm flbm mmm fmm,"
said Dragon.

Finally, Dragon wrapped himself up
just like a mummy.
Dragon hoped his costume would not be
too scary.

Dragon walked through the woods
to the big costume party.
Suddenly the wind began to blow.

"FLASH!" went the lightning.
"BOOM!" went the thunder.
And DOWN came the rain.

When Dragon finally got to the party,
he was soaking wet,
and his costume was ruined.
All of the animals began to laugh.

"Look at Dragon," they cried.
"Oh, what a silly costume!"

The animals laughed and laughed,
and Dragon felt terrible.
He walked over to a bench in the corner
and sat down next to a big pumpkin.

Suddenly, the bench broke,
and the pumpkin flipped high
into the air.

SPLAT!

Dragon was very dizzy.
He stumbled around the room
covered with slimy orange pumpkin goop.
When the animals saw Dragon,
they screamed in terror.

"*Eek!* It's a monster!" cried the duck,
who jumped into the pig's arms.

"Oh, dear! Oh, dear!" cried the pig,
who jumped into the hippo's arms.

"Help! Help! Help!" cried the hippo,
who jumped into the hamster's arms.

Finally, Dragon pulled the pumpkin
off his head.

"I am not a monster," said Dragon.
"I am only Dragon."

The animals were very relieved,
and soon everyone felt much better.

Well . . . *almost* everyone.

3

The Deep Dark Woods

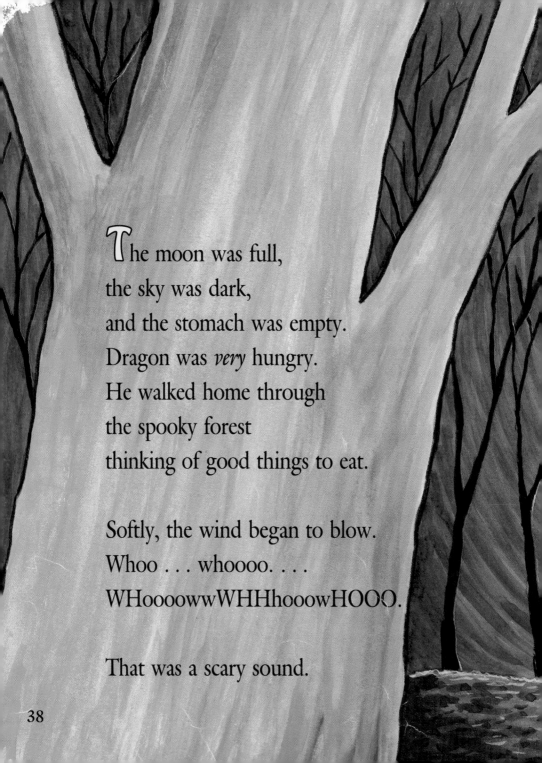

The moon was full,
the sky was dark,
and the stomach was empty.
Dragon was *very* hungry.
He walked home through
the spooky forest
thinking of good things to eat.

Softly, the wind began to blow.
Whoo . . . whoooo. . . .
WHoooowwWHHhoooowHOOO.

That was a scary sound.

The wet leaves beneath Dragon's feet
went *squish, squish, squish, squish!*

That was a scarier sound.

When Dragon got further into the forest,
he heard the scariest sound of all.

"Grrr . . . . . grrr . . . . . GRROWWWL!"

For a moment, everything was silent.
Then suddenly,

"Grrr . . . . . grrrr . . . . . GRRROWWWWL!"

"What could that awful noise be?"
cried Dragon.

"Grrrrr . . . grrrrr . . . GRRRROWWWWWL!"
The growling got louder and louder.

"GRRRR . . . GRRRRRRRRR . . .
GRRRRRRROWWWWWWWWWWWWL!"

Finally, Dragon jumped in the air.
"Help me!" he screamed.
"It's a *monster*!"

41

High up in the treetops,
a light flicked on.

"What's going on down there?"
shouted a sleepy-eyed squirrel.

"I hear a monster growling!"
cried Dragon.

"That's no monster," yelled the squirrel.
"That's your *stomach*!"

"Now go home and get something to eat
before you wake up the whole forest!"
cried the angry squirrel.

Dragon held his stomach.
It rumbled and growled.
He felt very silly.

All at once, the forest was dark again.
But now, Dragon was too hungry
to be afraid.
He ran and ran all the way home.

When Dragon got home,
he cooked up a giant Halloween feast.
He made pumpkin pies,
pumpkin soup,
pumpkin bread,
pumpkin pizzas,
and pumpkin ice-cream sundaes.

Then, Dragon ate and ate
and ate . . .

. . . until he was as round as a pumpkin.